LA GOUVERNEURE GÉNÉRALE
THE GOVERNOR GENERAL

What a beautiful story this is of Khadija, her brother Hamza and her parents, Abugee and Amigee. Khadija makes me think of myself when I arrived in Canada with my family. It had become dangerous for us to remain in Haiti, my country of birth, and my parents wanted my sister and me to have a better life, far from the violence and the misery.

I was 10 years old when we joined our father, who had arrived a little before us, like Khadija's dad. It was the middle of winter. I was coming from a country where the sun always shines; I didn't know what snow and cold were. What a shock! Also, my family and I were very different from the people who lived in the city where we settled. We were the only ones with dark skin, and that aroused a lot of curiosity.

Can I let you in on a secret? It took me some time to get used to my new life. But once I went to school, I understood the gift that my parents had given me. That's when I discovered how big the world is, and how full it is of possibilities. My grandmother always said, "Education, my children, is the key to freedom." She was right. The more educated we are, the more choices are available to us. The more you know, the more freedom you will have to choose and to live your dreams. And if there is a country big enough to hold all your dreams, it's Canada.

This country is your country. It's up to you to give it your imagination, your talent, your view of the world. And you know what? I believe that nothing is impossible for children like you and like Khadija and Hamza, who have courage, heart and a head brimming with ideas.

I hope your life in Canada is a wonderful adventure!

Michaëlle Jean

Coming to Canada

Rukhsana Khan

PICTURES BY

Nasrin Khosravi

GROUNDWOOD BOOKS   HOUSE OF ANANSI PRESS
TORONTO

Text copyright © 2008 by Rukhsana Khan
Appendix text copyright © 2008 by Settlement Workers in Schools
Illustrations copyright © 2008 by Nasrin Khosravi
Published in Canada in 2008 by Groundwood Books
Second printing 2010

Groundwood Books / House of Anansi Press
110 Spadina Avenue, Suite 801, Toronto, Ontario M5V 2K4

This book was produced with funding from the Government of Canada,
through Citizenship and Immigration Canada.

Canada

We acknowledge for their financial support of our publishing program the
Government of Canada through the Canada Book Fund (CBF).

Library and Archives Canada Cataloguing in Publication
Khan, Rukhsana
Coming to Canada / Rukhsana Khan; illustrated by Nasrin
Khosravi.
ISBN-13: 978-0-88899-879-8
ISBN-10: 0-88899-879-1
I. Khosravi, Nasrin II. Title.
PS8571.H42C65 2008   jC813'.54   C2007-907654-8

PICTURE CREDITS

Page 1: Sgt. Éric Jolin, Rideau Hall; Pages 49-54: All images courtesy
of Settlement Workers in Schools unless otherwise stated;
page 50: *Top* courtesy of the Government of Ontario, *center* Yellow Dog
Productions; page 53: All images courtesy of Masterfile – *top, left to right,*
© Dale Wilson, © Noel Hendrickson, © Dale Wilson, © Janet Foster,
© Dale Wilson, © Dale Wilson, © Didier Dorval, *bottom, left to right,*
© Roy Ooms, © Alec Pytolwany, © Mike Macri, © Greg Stott,
© J.A. Kraulis, © Greg Stott; page 55: Arms of Canada reproduced with the
permission of the Government of Canada, 2008.

Design by Michael Solomon
Maps by Leon Grek
Printed and bound in Canada

CHAPTER ONE

Saying Goodbye

A NEW LAND. A new country. A new home. How exciting!

But Hamza doesn't think so.

"Why do we have to go?" says Hamza.

My father puts down his suitcase and touches Hamza's cheek. "For the schools, the opportunities. I'm doing this for you. Now give me a hug."

Hamza turns away, but Abugee pulls him into his arms and squeezes him tight. When he lets go I can see that Hamza is smiling in spite of himself. Then it's my turn. My father's big arms circle me like a thick blanket and he kisses the top of my head.

"You be good for your mother, Khadija. Insha Allah, I'll see you soon. In Canada!"

He sounds excited.

My mother has tears in her eyes. Abugee nods at her and Amigee nods back, pulling her chador close.

Abugee has to bend down to kiss my grandmother.

Daddiami rubs the top of his head. And then he's gone, to set up a house for us in Canada.

Hamza runs up the stairs and slams the door to his room. A look passes between my mother and grandmother, and then Daddiami follows after him. She walks up the stairs slowly. I could pass her if I wanted to, but I hang back.

Hamza's lying face down on the bed. Is he crying?

Daddiami says, "For shame, Hamza. Stop carrying on. Look at Khadija. How brave she is!"

I grin up at her but Daddiami doesn't notice. She goes onto the veranda. What's she doing out there? I can hear some pots being moved around. Hamza is curious too, and we peek at her from the doorway.

"Come see this."

She's fussing with the jasmine bush. "This plant is too crowded," she says. "There's no room for the young shoots to grow."

She pulls out a little stem that was hiding beneath some of the leaves and pushes it into its own pot of black earth. She pats the soil around it so it's good and firm, then picks up the can of water to give it a drink.

"When a plant is young, it is easy to move," Daddiami says. "It takes time, but eventually it gets used to its new place. New roots will grow and new leaves will sprout. It's difficult to move a mature plant and you cannot move a plant that is old. You'll only kill it. It will miss the soil it grew up in and die of homesickness.

"It will be hard for your parents, even harder than it will be for you. You must be strong. And you must make it easy for them. I'm counting on you."

CHAPTER TWO
The Arrival

THIS NEW country of Canada is cold, but at least it's raining. I've always liked the rain. It doesn't rain much in Pakistan.

Hamza's in a foul mood. He misses Daddiami. So do I, but that doesn't mean I can't be excited too.

There is so much to look at as we wait in line with our passports. The people are so tall. And they're dressed so stylishly, their hair clipped neatly.

The lady officer we report to is wearing lots of make-up and she has fluffy yellow hair. I wish I could touch it. I wonder what it feels like.

I don't like the way she looks at Amigee. It makes me see her in a different way. I never noticed how shabby Amigee looks. But that's from the flight, isn't it? Hamza said we sat for sixteen hours. All the passengers look shabby, don't they?

The fancy doors open sideways when we get close to them. I barely have time to wonder how they knew we were coming, because I see Abugee pressed against the barrier on the other side.

He looks older. I'm sure there is more grey hair at the sides of his face. But when he wraps me in his big arms, it feels exactly the same.

I can't wait to see our new home. I've seen pictures of houses in North America on TV. They're always clean and fashionable.

But the house that Abugee has set up for us isn't even

a house. It's an apartment, just a few rooms. And the furniture isn't new. It has scratches and dents.

Abugee looks sorry. "One day we'll have money to buy whatever we want," he promises Amigee.

Hamza wrinkles up his nose at it, but I think my bed is real bouncy.

⁂ ⁂ ⁂

The very next day Amigee takes us to the school to register. She struggles to speak English, but the lady at the desk goes over to an office that has a sign on the door and calls, "Mrs. Shankar!"

That sounds Indian and Mrs. Shankar is Indian, but when she comes towards us she looks strange and uncomfortable. She's wearing the same kind of clothes as the lady at the desk, but they're rumpled and too tight.

Hamza nudges me. "Who does she think she is?" Amigee squeezes his arm and he is quiet.

Mrs. Shankar's accent is different from ours but at least we can understand her. "Good morning. I'm the vice-principal. Welcome to our school. Have you brought your documents? We need your landed immigrant papers, immunization records and birth certificates. And do you have health card numbers and a copy of a bill to prove that you live in the area?"

We don't have most of those papers, so Amigee has to call Abugee and he uses his taxi to take us around to get them. First we go to get our health cards, then this place, then that place with lots of standing in line. The next day we visit the doctor's office where we get some needles. Ow!

On our first day of school I get up extra early. Hamza's already in the bathroom. The nice thing about Canada is that there's always hot water in the taps. Abugee says there's lots of water here and we can take as many showers as we want. Hamza takes too long though. I bang on the door and yell, "Have you turned into a fish?"

Hamza doesn't even answer.

Finally, the door opens. I wash quickly, clean my teeth and brush my hair. I put on some socks. They feel funny on my feet, but Abugee says we have to get used to wearing them. Then I gulp down my breakfast. I put on my coat and boots. Hamza's still munching his toast.

Amigee riffles through the papers making sure we have everything and then we walk to school. By the time Mrs. Shankar has helped us fill out all the forms, classes have already started.

Amigee bends down to hug and kiss us. "Be good," she says, mostly to Hamza.

Hamza doesn't answer. He just looks down at the floor. Amigee pushes his chin up with her knuckle and looks right into his eyes. "You be good."

Hamza nods and Amigee stands up straight and walks to the big front door. She looks back at us only once and then leaves.

The principal walks us down the hall. It's so empty. It feels like we're the only ones in the school. Her high heels echo on the clean bare floor. The school looks old and shabby. I thought it would be sparkling new, but I guess this is an older part of town.

We go to Hamza's class first because it's closer. They put him in grade five.

The principal knocks and there are fluttery feelings in my stomach. Did Hamza just gulp? He must be nervous too.

The door opens and the principal walks into a bright room. The windows are huge, stretching up almost to the ceiling, and at first the light is all I can see.

And then I see all the faces staring at us. Nobody looks like us. The principal is talking to the teacher and the students. I think she's introducing us, but it sounds like this: "Gudmor ning clas deezar nu stoodens HAMZA und KHADIJA. I hope yool maycdem walcum."

Hamza whispers, "They look like they want to eat me."

"Ssh," I say. "A few of them are smiling."

Then the principal takes me away to my classroom, and the last thing I see as the door closes is Hamza's worried face.

Now it's my turn. My hands are sweaty.

When we get to my classroom the principal smiles and says, "Dis iz yonu clas room. I hope yoolbee hapee heer."

She's waiting for me to say something, so I just nod and then she opens the door.

Phew! There must be a big difference between these

grade three kids and grade five kids, because the faces look pretty friendly.

I hear the principal say my name and all the kids look at me. Then she says, "I wan evree wun toobee nis tooer." And she says some other stuff too, and then she leaves.

The teacher, Ms. Thomson, hands me a textbook and takes me to sit beside a pretty girl with a pink ribbon in her hair. By the way the girl points and nudges me I figure out I'm supposed to open my textbook.

I look at the pictures while Ms. Thomson starts her lesson.

Abugee liked taking us places when we lived in Pakistan. We drove all over the country. He liked the old places best. He would teach us history as we looked at the beautiful buildings the Moghuls had built. The first time he took us to the Shalimar Gardens it was a hot sunny day and people were splashing in the pools to cool off.

I was little then and I begged so hard that Amigee finally let me go into one of the pools with Hamza. I had to tiptoe to touch the bottom. I kept my neck stretched up just so I could breathe. When people splashed I got a mouthful of water and started to cough. It was scary but I didn't want Amigee to take me out, so I pretended everything was fine.

That feeling of not being able to swim and hardly

being able to touch the bottom is kind of how I feel as I try to learn English. I can hardly understand what people are saying. In Ms. Thomson's class, they talk so fast. Every once in a while they say a word I know. But by the time I realize it, they've moved on to say something else.

In the afternoon I am pulled out of the class with two other girls. One girl is about my colour. We go to a special teacher named Mrs. Baker to learn to speak English.

From the first moment, I love Mrs. Baker. She's so gentle. She talks nice and slow, and she always gives me a chance to think of how to answer. There are eight other kids in our class.

We point at ourselves and say our names. The two girls from my class are Margarita and Rada. Margarita is from Nicaragua and Rada is from Somalia.

I've never seen hair like Rada's. It's fuzzy, like wool. I want to touch it, but I've learned it's not polite.

On the way home I see Margarita and Rada walking ahead. They turn right into the walkway of our own building. It turns out that Margarita lives on the fifth floor and Rada's on the eleventh.

That night at supper I tell my parents about my new friends.

Abugee takes out his atlas and we look for Nicaragua and Somalia, and then we find Pakistan. They're so far apart. With our fingers we trace a line across the oceans, across the different-coloured countries, all the way here to Canada. It's a long way.

Abugee says there are many people from all over the world in this country. How do they all get along?

CHAPTER THREE

School Days

A WEEK HAS passed and I'm starting to get used to the school schedule, but I still jump when the recess bell rings. It sounds so shrill and loud. The other kids don't even flinch. In fact they look happy, so I try to pretend I'm not nervous.

First the teacher makes us line up at a white boxy thing that sticks out of the wall. It has a knob on the side that you turn and a little shiny part at the top where water squirts out. All the other kids are eager to stick their tongues in the water, and they linger so the teacher has to count their turn – 1, 2, 3… I try to look eager too, but what good is wetting your tongue? I wish I had a cup. I could angle it towards that stream of water and fill it up. I'd just love a drink of water!

When we get out into the yard the kids are running and screaming, bouncing balls and skipping rope.

Where's Hamza? There are so many children, it's hard to see him. He's not by the sandbox, not by the grassy field.

There he is by the corner of the school building. He's

got his hands shoved in his pockets and a scowl on his face.

He says, "These people with their fancy clothes and their expensive shoes and the way they look down their noses at you because you don't have those things yet."

"Not everyone's like that. Some of them have been nice to me."

"That's because you're only in grade three. Wait till you get to my age. Then you'll see the way they really are."

A big girl runs by to catch a ball but she stops when she sees us. "Hamza!"

She calls over her shoulder to the others. They talk a bit, then one of them nods. "C'mon," she says.

I take a step forward and she glances at me but doesn't tell me "no," so I guess I can go too.

They're playing a weird kind of cricket. But their bat isn't flat, it's round like a broomstick. And there's no wicket. And they don't bowl the ball. They throw it over a flat thing on the ground. Hamza's playing in the field. I get to chase down the stray balls.

When the bell rings I wait for Hamza to catch up. "See? They're being nice to you. They let you play."

"I didn't get to bat."

"Maybe your team didn't have a turn yet."

"Didn't you see them change? The other team told me to stay out in the field too."

"Maybe they thought you'd rather field."

Hamza gives me a look like I've said something really silly.

⊛   ⊛   ⊛

The next day I spend recess trying to cheer up Hamza again. When the same girl calls him to play, Hamza points at the bat and makes a move to show he wants to swing it.

The girl frowns and points to the outfield. Hamza crosses his arms and leans against the side of the school.

"See?" Hamza says. "They're never going to let me bat. Did you see the way those guys looked at me?"

I nod. It wasn't very nice. Maybe Hamza is right.

He says, "They think we're poor, just because we don't have fancy stuff like they have. They think we're not as good as they are."

"But we're not poor," I say. "We had nice things in Pakistan. Don't they know we can't afford them right now? It's just going to take time, like Daddiami said."

"I'm tired of waiting."

Margarita and Rada come towards me. They have a skipping rope. It must have broken because there's a big fat knot in the middle. Maybe it'll be hard to jump over that knot, but I'd still like to try.

I look over at Hamza. Will he mind?

Hamza's scowling again. "Why don't you just go with your *friends*. Leave me alone."

Does he mean it? But then I see his bottom lip quivering. I look away before Hamza sees that I'm staring. In Pakistan, he was the one who loved school and had lots of friends.

Rada nudges me with the skipping rope. I shake my

head and step closer to Hamza. Rada turns and goes off with Margarita. I wish I could go with them.

For a while Hamza and I watch the other kids play, but it gets boring real fast. We can't just stand here all recess. So I ask, "Do you have Mrs. Baker for English too?"

"What do you think?"

"I'm just asking!"

"What a stupid question. Who else would I have? All the kids who can't speak English have to go to her."

We're quiet for a few moments. Hamza glares at the kids playing that game then he says, "I bet they don't know I can read. And I even know a few words in English. I bet they think I'm dumb. I'd like to show them!"

"Stop it!"

Hamza looks surprised.

"Just stop it." And for once he does. For the rest of recess we stand there watching all the other kids play. He doesn't say one word, but his temper is boiling up inside. I can tell.

The bell rings and we march back into the school. One of the kids in Hamza's class is right beside him. He looks mean, and he says something but I can't hear it.

Then Hamza stops by a little red box that's stuck on the wall. That kid from his class says something to him again. There are words written on the little red box in white letters. Hamza stands in front of it with all the other kids jostling past him and reads "P-U-L-L." Pull. So he does.

Immediately a different bell starts ringing. It's very loud and urgent, and the teachers look scared. The mean kid laughs. The teachers yell something and tell everyone to go back outside. We line up in rows according to our classes.

The principal comes storming out, talking to the teachers. Then that mean kid in Hamza's class, the one who told him to do it, points right at him. The tattletale.

In front of the whole school Hamza's teacher Mr. Oyoung pulls him forward to face the principal. They call Mrs. Shankar to join them too. Are they going to beat Hamza? His face is red. He's standing so still, like he's turned into a statue.

Mrs. Shankar speaks to the principal quietly. Her eyes grow wide and she stares at Hamza.

I can't stand it any longer. I run towards Mrs. Shankar yelling, "It was an accident. He didn't know!"

Mrs. Shankar tells me to go back to my place in line. Rada puts an arm around me, and I feel a little better.

Then Mrs. Shankar bends close to Hamza and says, "You pulled the fire alarm. It's against the rules. You can't do that. You mustn't ever do that again. Okay?"

Hamza's face is so serious. He nods and then he says quietly, "Are you going to tell my parents?"

Mrs. Shankar frowns. "No. I don't think that's necessary. Just don't ever do that again. Not unless there's a fire. Okay?"

Hamza nods. And one by one the teachers file their classes back into the school.

That's it? No beating? They didn't even yell at him. But maybe they're saving it for when he gets back to the classroom.

All afternoon in Mrs. Baker's class I try not to worry, but it's hard.

I can't wait to see if Hamza's all right. When he comes out of his class he looks fine. I don't see any bruises and he's not crying.

I can't ask Hamza while we're walking home with Amigee. And I can't ask him at dinnertime. It's not until we're tucked into our beds that I can ask him what happened.

"Nothing," he says. "What you saw. That was it."

"But what about the other kids? Didn't they make fun of you?"

"Nope. That's the strangest thing. They started being nice to me. Really nice."

"But you're not going to pull the alarm again, are you?"

"Of course not! I wouldn't have done it the first time if I'd known what it was."

The very next day that same girl asks Hamza to play again, and this time they let him swing the bat. Hamza swings three times without hitting the ball, and they tell him he's "out" and has to give the next person a turn. When the teams change, he goes back to playing outfield, but this time he doesn't seem to mind. He even looks a bit happier.

About a week later, we arrive home after a long day of school. We haven't even taken our coats off when Amigee says, "What have you done?" She's staring at Hamza. Did she find out about the fire alarm?

Hamza's face turns red and he looks at the floor.

"Tell me right now and you won't get into so much trouble with your father."

I hold my breath, waiting for Hamza to tell, but instead he shrugs. "I didn't do anything."

Amigee looks doubtful. Hamza looks straight up at her without blinking. For a few moments they just stand there, frozen. And then, finally, Amigee turns away. "Never mind," she says. We'll find out soon enough. Your teacher called and we have to meet him tonight."

Amigee calls Mrs. Korczak from next door to look after us. And then she goes into the kitchen to begin supper. We can finally take off our coats.

Hamza looks worried. I nudge him and say, "Do you think it's about the fire alarm?"

"I don't think so. They said they wouldn't tell, and even if they were going to, they wouldn't have waited this long."

When Abugee hears the news his face gets dark and he stares at Hamza. "What did you do?"

"Nothing."

"Then why would they call? You must have done something."

"No. I've been good."

"Are you lying?"

"No, Abugee. Honest."

"We'll see about that."

Mrs. Korczak comes over after supper. She takes off her shawl and hangs it on the hook. Then she plops down in front of the TV.

"We won't be long," calls Amigee.

Mrs. Korczak cups her hand around her ear. "Eh?"

"WE WON'T BE LONG!"

Mrs. Korczak nods and turns back to the TV.

When the door closes behind them, Hamza says, "Let's go to bed before they get back. They can't yell at me if I'm asleep. They'll have to wait till tomorrow, and by then they won't be so angry. If it is anything."

"But *did* you do something?" I ask.

Hamza scowls. "NO!"

"Okay, okay. I was just wondering."

We get all ready for bed. Hamza sits near the window, glancing down at the street for any sign of our parents. In the middle of a really funny show, he cries, "They're coming."

We rush into the bedroom. Lights out, try to get to bed. Ow! I bumped my shin!

"Sssh!" says Hamza.

I pull up the covers just as the key turns in the lock. They're talking quietly. Amigee is saying what a nice walk it was. Abugee is agreeing with her. Then Amigee says, "THANK YOU VERY MUCH, MRS. KORCZAK!" And pretty soon the door closes behind her. Now will they start yelling?

Abugee says, "Hamza?"

"Ssh. They're sleeping," Amigee says. And look, they didn't forget to do their chores."

The light from the hallway casts their shadows across my blankets and against the wall.

Amigee says, "They really are very good, don't you think?"

"His teacher said so. How can we argue?"

Amigee says, "We'll show him the extra work Mr. Oyoung wants him to do tomorrow."

Quietly they shut the door.

I whisper, "Hamza? You awake?"

"Yeah."

"Did you hear that?"

"Yeah."

"Doesn't sound like they're mad at all."

"See? Told you I was good."

He rolls over, and in a few moments I can hear him breathing heavily.

CHAPTER FOUR
A Dragon in a Book

MONTHS HAVE gone by. I know quite a bit of English now. So does Hamza. I only spend an hour in Mrs. Baker's class these days, not the whole afternoon. She's teaching me how to read English properly. In Pakistan, we learned the alphabet and how to read a few words, so it's not too hard. Especially now that I know what most of the words mean.

Today Mrs. Baker has a surprise for me. It's a big brown box with some writing on the side.

"Open it," she says.

"What's inside?"

"You'll see."

I struggle with the tape till she hands me a pair of scissors. I pull out the packing material to find a pile of books. Special books just for me and Hamza, where the story is written in English and Urdu!

Mrs. Baker already has some books with Somali for Rada, and some with Spanish for Margarita and even some with other languages.

She says, "Why don't you read to us?"

The English words are a bit hard. I struggle to sound them out. Mrs. Baker says, "No, no. Read it in Urdu."

"But you won't understand."

"Okay, I'll read the English and then you read the Urdu."

And so we read together and I do my best. Rada and Margarita and the other kids all listen carefully. Then Mrs. Baker takes a turn with Margarita reading her English and Spanish book.

Mrs. Baker lets me borrow my book. She wants Amigee to read it to me in Urdu tonight.

A few weeks later, Mrs. Baker takes us to the school library. Today I'm going to pick a chapter book. I find one with a picture of a shiny gold dragon on the cover. I take it to the table and open it to the first page.

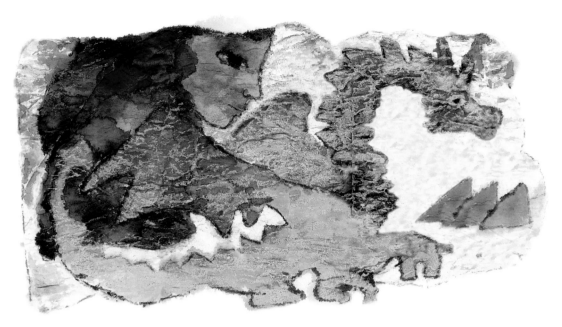

I sound out the words like Mrs. Baker showed me: "The dra-gon flew o-ver the moun-tain and…" All of a sudden the words on the page disappear, and I can see a dragon beating its wings!

Am I going crazy? I shake my head and look up. It breaks the spell.

The dragon's gone. I'm back here, in the school library. There's Mrs. Baker helping Margarita choose a book, and there's Rada reading something about a kitten. Okay. Let's try this again.

"The dragon flew over the mountain and saw a village surrounded by a dark forest."

Again the words vanish and I see a dragon and a village.

Does this happen to everyone, or is it just me? I read it again and this time I don't stop.

Wow! Reading a book is like making a movie in my head, and I'm the star. Well, actually, right now I'm a dragon.

I swear it's magical!

✳ ✳ ✳

Abugee has gotten grumpy. Maybe he's tired. He drives a taxi during the day, and then he has to go to school at night and on weekends. Sometimes I hear him grumble. Some of his customers are mean to him.

He's waiting to get his university degree from Pakistan approved. So many rules and regulations, he says. And he has to go to school to improve his English so he can be a substitute teacher, even though he was a principal back in

Pakistan. If he can just get his teacher's certificate, things will be better.

Today Hamza and I make too much noise when he is trying to sleep. He yells at us and then stomps back to bed. I bump Hamza with one of his cars but he shoos me away. He says he is thinking up a plan to make Abugee happy.

When Abugee finally gets up, Hamza says, "Can we go to the library? My teacher says it has all kinds of interesting stuff."

Abugee's eyes light up. It was the perfect thing for Hamza to say. Amigee says she'll come too.

The library isn't very far so we walk. Abugee is happy to be out of his taxi. The library is in a big building. Inside it is very tidy with wall-to-wall carpet and some people at computers and others reading quietly at desks.

Abugee gestures to all the books. "Here you see the real treasure of this country."

Hamza wrinkles his forehead. "Books?"

"Not just books! Knowledge! This is why we came here. This will help us make a better life. This library contains all the best information you can find. And it's available to everyone in the land, both rich and poor. And it's free."

Abugee takes Hamza to look at the non-fiction section. Hamza wants to know about sharks and dinosaurs and hockey. I go over to the chapter books and get one about a beautiful horse.

Even Amigee chooses a book. It's in Urdu. That's so nice of them to have books that we can read.

By the time we go home, Abugee is in a much better mood.

I show Hamza the book I got. He doesn't look that interested, so I say, "You know what? When I read in English something magical happens!" And I tell him about the movie in my head.

Hamza says, "Don't be silly! It's not magic. It happens when you read Urdu books too." Then he picks up one of the books we brought with us from Pakistan and tells me to start reading.

He's right! The pictures form in the very same way.

"How come I didn't see them before?"

"You have to get good enough at reading first."

He makes it sound so ordinary!

Never mind. I still think it's magical.

⁎ ⁎ ⁎

While I am waiting to walk home with Hamza, some bully kids call me dirty names. It makes me cry. When Hamza sees me he knows something is wrong. He makes me tell him about it. He gets so mad. "Show me them," he says.

They are in the sandbox.

Hamza starts marching towards them. I pull at his shirt saying, "Just ignore them."

But he won't. He chases them down and there's a shoving match. It's two against one, but Hamza still manages to scare them.

The school calls home and Hamza gets in trouble. Abugee yells at him, telling him he's throwing away his chances. Amigee looks sad. Hamza just sits there and listens. He doesn't tell them it was all because of me.

When they're done and he's promised not to fight again, he comes into our room. "Are you okay?" I say.

He shrugs.

"Thanks."

He looks at me then. "No problem," he says.

It's true that our home is much shabbier than in Pakistan, but even here there are those who have it worse. Margarita's apartment is a lot like ours, but it's much smaller. And it smells different. Her mom gave me a burrito with beans and salad inside. It was delicious.

After I bug Rada for a long time, she finally gets permission for me to visit. Rada's house smells different too. She lives in a two-bedroom apartment like ours, but instead of sharing a room with a brother, she doesn't even have a room. Her uncle's family has one bedroom, and her mother and father and baby brother have the other. Rada sleeps with her sister in the living room on a sofa that turns into a bed at night.

"Where's your study area?" I ask.

Rada looks at me like I said something weird.

Rada's mother looks very tired. She works as an assistant cook in a senior citizens' home even though she was a nurse and midwife back in Somalia.

"Let's go find Margarita and we can play ball downstairs," I say.

Rada looks doubtful but she goes to her mother and asks anyway. Her mother glances at me but shakes her head. "You know it's too dangerous."

It's not dangerous!

Rada sighs. "She never lets me out of the apartment except to go to school."

When I tell Amigee what Rada's mom said, I expect her to laugh, but she doesn't.

Amigee says, "She's right. It isn't safe."

Abugee says, "It isn't that bad. There are problems everywhere."

Amigee agrees, and they are both silent for a while. Finally, Abugee says, "Some people have come from places where there was war. Maybe they are too scared to let their children out of their sight."

I invite Rada and Margarita to my house but Rada isn't allowed to come. She has to help take care of her baby brother. When Margarita arrives we make our own kind of burritos with some of our rotis and a bit of minced beef cooked in Pakistani spices.

Margarita takes a big bite and says, "Rotis and tortillas are practically the same thing."

I think she's right.

{*}   {*}   {*}

It's close to the end of the school year and the days are hot and sticky. Especially today and I'm so thirsty. I'd do anything for a cup so I could get a drink of water. It's recess time and I'm so desperate, I'm even eager to line up and wet my tongue in the water fountain.

It's finally my turn. Somehow I breathe in when the stream of water touches my lips. The water! It goes right into my mouth, just like drinking from a cup!

So that's what this thing is for! They weren't just wetting their tongues. They were actually drinking the water!

Gulp, gulp, gulp!

"1, 2, 3 . . . next!" But I still want more. This time I'm the one they nudge to let the next kid have a turn. But at least I'll never be thirsty at school again!

CHAPTER FIVE

Now for the Rest of Canada

I'M IN GRADE five now and it's my turn to have Mr. Oyoung as a teacher. He's nice but gives us way too much homework. I hardly see Mrs. Baker at all except when I go downstairs after school to visit her.

There are new kids who've come to the school from countries far away. When I see them looking so nervous and scared, it makes me remember how I felt and I try to be nice to them.

One day when we get home from school Abugee is already there. He looks tired and happy at the same time. "It's a wonderful day," he tells us. "I just got my teacher's certificate!"

"Does this mean no more taxi?" Amigee asks.

Abugee shakes his head. "No, the money is good. But now I can substitute teach as well. It's a way to get my foot in the door."

Abugee worked so hard and he only has his foot in the door? How long will it take before he gets his whole self in?

After that Abugee works twice as hard. He wants to make enough money to buy a house.

Amigee decides to help. She gets a job at a coffee shop. The first day of work she wears her uniform: a pair of pants and a shirt. The clothes are kind of tight, and Amigee looks a bit uncomfortable, just like Mrs. Shankar.

Hamza stares at Amigee but doesn't say one word.

{*} {*} {*}

When Abugee finally gets his first full-time job as a teacher, he quits being a taxi driver. To celebrate, Abugee and Amigee decide to take us on a trip before the next school year begins.

Abugee trades in the taxi for a mini van, the kind where the seats fold underneath and we can sleep on the floor. We're going to drive all the way to the Yukon to see some of this big new country of ours.

We drive up through the forests of Ontario to the flat grass prairies of Manitoba and Saskatchewan, where breezes ripple through fields like waves on the ocean.

Canada is so vast. It takes us a week just to get to Calgary. Hamza knows the names of some of the towns we pass through because his favourite hockey players come from there.

We first catch a glimpse of the Rocky Mountains in Alberta. Their sharp peaks poke the sky and have snow on them, even in the summertime. Those mountains keep us company all the way up the coast of British Columbia.

In the Yukon there is so much purple fireweed. We see moose and even bears right by the side of the road! And when we shut off the engine, the silence presses against our ears.

We stop at all kinds of museums and shops. On the main road in Whitehorse we meet a Native family: a mother, father and brother and sister, kind of like us. They look at us and we look at them. They smile at us and we smile at them. And then we nod and they nod back, and we go on our way.

The next summer we go down east, to Nova Scotia and New Brunswick, and then up north to Newfoundland. Hamza likes the ferry ride to Newfoundland. We see icebergs in the water and know it's too cold to swim. The best is when we go whale watching. Hamza is the first to spot a dark grey whale when it comes up to breathe. He cries, "Thar she blows!" just like they do in the movies we've seen. All the other tourists laugh.

Even Hamza has to admit that this country is amazing.

When we get back it feels like our apartment has shrunk, or maybe it's me who has grown.

✻ ✻ ✻

Years have passed and things have changed. We got our citizenship papers at a special ceremony with a judge and everything. We really are Canadian now. We have every right to be here and the exact same rights as any other Canadian.

Hamza joined a junior hockey league. Abugee bought him used equipment. He's a great defenseman.

We have a house now with a veranda that Daddiami would love. We put some plants on it, just like she did in Pakistan.

She's coming to visit, and we're cleaning and painting and making the place look its very best for her arrival. Still, there's something missing.

Amigee drives me to the big department store. "What is it you want, Khadija?" she says.

I shrug. I'll know it when I see it.

Up and down the aisles past wallpaper and ceramic tiles, something pulls me towards the garden section. And then I see it. A little jasmine plant. It's perfect.

A jasmine plant growing in a shop in Canada!

It even has some buds on it. I bet they will open by the time Daddiami comes.

THE END

Glossary

Abugee: father

Amigee: mother

Burrito: tortilla stuffed with meat or beans

Chador: shawl

Daddiami: grandmother (father's mother)

Insha Allah: Arabic phrase meaning "if God wills"

Moghuls: dynasty of Muslim rulers, beginning with Babur and ending
    with Aurangzeb, who ruled India from the sixteenth to the begin-
    ning of the eighteenth centuries. They were most famous for their
    beautiful style of architecture, which includes the Taj Mahal and
    the Shalimar Gardens.

Roti: Indian bread (thin flat bread)

Shalimar Gardens: three terraced gardens in Lahore, Pakistan, which
    date back to the Moghul empire

Tortilla: Hispanic bread (thin flat bread)

Urdu: one of the languages spoken in Pakistan and India

Are you new to Canada?

Coming to a new country can be a little overwhelming, but there are many free government and community services to help you. Many of these services are provided by settlement agencies. To locate the settlement agency closest to your home, see www.settlement.org. Many schools and libraries have settlement workers who can also help you understand how schools and libraries work. Avoid frustration and use these free services.

SUCCESS IN SCHOOL

Starting school in a new country can be hard. Children need to make new friends, adjust to new teachers and to a new school. Many are learning a new language. Teachers will make the transition as easy as possible, but there are many ways that parents can help too. Here are some suggestions.

• **Talk to your child about school**. Choose a quiet time every day or so to ask, "What happened at school?" Talking about the day's events helps you understand what is going well and what might be difficult for your child. It also helps you learn about the school and gives you a chance to offer advice and support.

• **Attend parent-teacher interviews.** Once or twice a year, parents are expected to meet their child's teacher. The teacher will tell you how your child is doing and what you can do to help him or her to do well. Some schools can provide an interpreter, or you can bring a friend who speaks English. See the video about parent-teacher interviews at www.SWISOntario.ca. It is available in 17 languages.

• **Contact the teacher if you have a question or concern**. Parents sometimes need to talk to the teacher about school work, their child's relationship with another student or other concerns. Teachers are accustomed to talking with parents in between parent-teacher interviews. When necessary, ask to meet the teacher or speak on the phone.

The Settlement.Org website provides comprehensive, useful and up-to-date information and resources to help new immigrants settle in Ontario. You will find information you can trust about housing, employment, health, learning English and much more. In addition, you will find information about childcare services and how to obtain the Canada Child Tax Benefit. The Resource Kit for New Immigrant Parents has information about learning, recreation, health and safety, and talking to your child. Settlement.Org has information in over 30 languages.

Pour des renseignements sur tous les aspects du processus d'établissement, visitez le site web www.etablissement.org.

• **Be aware of bullying.** Most children have occasional disagreements with other children at school. Usually these are resolved by the children themselves or with the help of the teacher. But sometimes one student or a group of students takes advantage of another student. If your child is very unhappy at school, or becomes afraid of going to school and won't tell you why, or if your child is losing things and can't tell you what happened, then those may be signs of bullying.

If you believe that your child is being bullied by another student, you should contact your child's teacher, even if your child does not want you to get involved.

To help parents, the Ontario Ministry of Education has produced information about bullying. It describes what parents can do and what they can expect from the school. It is available in 22 languages at www.edu.gov.on.ca/eng/parents/bullying.html.

• **Join the public library.** Public libraries are free and easy to join. To get a library card, all you have to do is go to the library with proof of your home address and a piece of identification. Library staff will prepare cards for you and your child while you wait so that you can borrow books and other materials on your first visit.

The library offers many services to help children succeed in school such as story-time for young children and books in many languages. Many students study, do homework and use the computers at the library. Library staff can help your child find information for school projects.

Many newcomers come to the library for books, computer access, DVDs, materials to learn English, programs for children and information about community services.

The library also has career information for adults and is a quiet, friendly place to think and plan your career path in Canada.

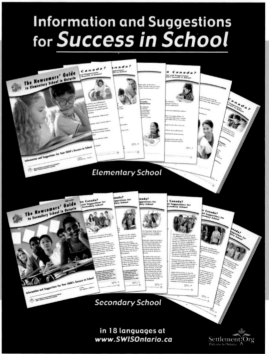

Children learn English at different rates, even two children in the same family. At first, children learn to speak English in day-to-day situations, but it can take five to seven years for a child to learn to speak, read, write and understand complex material at the same level as an English-speaking classmate. Often a child's speaking skills develop more quickly than his or her writing and reading skills. Children with good reading and writing skills in their first language learn to read and write English more quickly.

Your child may spend part of the school day with an "English as a Second Language" (ESL) teacher and the rest of the day with his or her classmates. The ESL teacher will help your child learn key English-language skills, while time in the regular classroom gives your child a chance to practice those skills. All children who are learning English go through a series of stages. Talk to your child's teacher about your child's stage and how you can help. For more information, see www.edu.gov.on.ca/eng/document/curricul/esl18.pdf.

To help your child learn English:

• **Continue talking to your child in your first language.** A strong foundation in their home language helps children succeed at school in English. Consider enrolling your child in after-school or weekend classes so that he or she can continue learning his or her first language while learning English. Public libraries have books in many languages so that students can continue to practice their reading skills. See www.icdlbooks.org for books in many languages. You can read them on a computer or download them.

• **Encourage your child to join group activities at lunchtime and after school.** Teachers supervise these activities, which give your child a chance to make friends and practice English.

• **Encourage your child to participate in discussions in class.** It takes courage and parental support for students to speak to the whole class.

If your child is not accustomed to a cold winter, you may be in for a surprise! Sometimes children need to learn how to dress for winter. This illustration will help your child enjoy his or her first winter in Canada. Watch the video at www.SWISOntario.ca.

Dressing For Winter

New to Canada?

10°
5°
0°
-10°
-15°
-20°

Hat   Jacket   Boots   Mittens

Snowsuit   Boots   Scarf

Hat   Sweater   Mittens

Settlement.Org Canada

Funded by Subventionné par Citizenship and Citoyenneté et Immigration Canada Immigration Canada

See the video: www.SWISOntario.ca

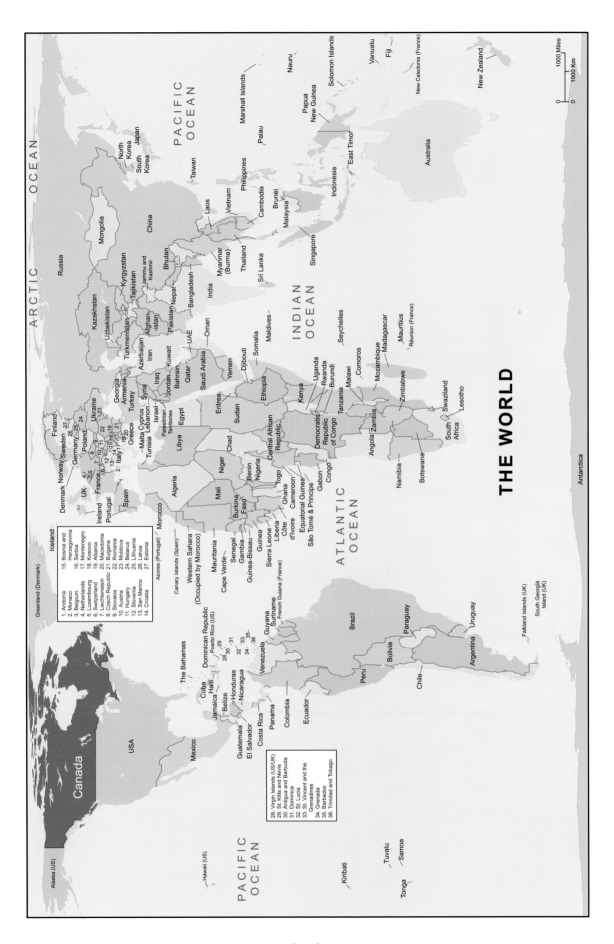

THE WORLD

PACIFIC OCEAN

ARCTIC OCEAN

ATLANTIC OCEAN

INDIAN OCEAN

Antarctica

1000 Miles

1000 Km

Greenland (Denmark)

Iceland

1. Andorra
2. Monaco
3. Belgium
4. Netherlands
5. Switzerland
6. Liechtenstein
7. Liechtenstein
8. Czech Republic
9. Slovakia
10. Austria
11. Hungary
12. Slovenia
13. San Marino
14. Croatia
15. Bosnia and Herzegovina
16. Serbia
17. Montenegro
18. Kosovo
19. Albania
20. Macedonia
21. Bulgaria
22. Romania
23. Moldova
24. Belarus
25. Lithuania
26. Latvia
27. Estonia

Azores (Portugal)

Canary Islands (Spain)

Western Sahara (Occupied by Morocco)

28. Virgin Islands (US/UK)
29. St. Kitts and Nevis
30. Antigua and Barbuda
31. Dominica
32. St. Lucia
33. St. Vincent and the Grenadines
34. Grenada
35. Barbados
36. Trinidad and Tobago

Canada

Alaska (US)

USA

Mexico

The Bahamas

Cuba
Jamaica
Belize
Guatemala
El Salvador
Honduras
Nicaragua
Costa Rica
Panama

Haiti
Dominican Republic
Puerto Rico (US)

Colombia
Ecuador
Venezuela
Guyana
Suriname
French Guiana (France)

Peru
Brazil
Bolivia
Paraguay
Chile
Argentina
Uruguay

Falkland Islands (UK)

South Georgia Island (UK)

Hawaii (US)

Kiribati
Tuvalu
Samoa
Tonga

Russia

Mongolia

Kazakhstan

Uzbekistan
Turkmenistan
Kyrgyzstan
Tajikistan

Finland
Norway
Sweden
Denmark
UK
Ireland
France
Portugal
Spain
Poland
Germany
Greece

China

North Korea
South Korea
Japan
Taiwan

Laos
Vietnam
Cambodia
Myanmar (Burma)
Thailand
Brunei
Malaysia
Singapore
Indonesia
Philippines
Palau

Marshall Islands
Nauru
Papua New Guinea
Solomon Islands
Vanuatu
Fiji
New Caledonia (France)
New Zealand

Australia

East Timor

Georgia
Armenia
Azerbaijan
Iran
Iraq
Turkey
Syria
Lebanon
Israel
Cyprus
Malta
Tunisia
Morocco

Afghanistan
Pakistan
Jammu and Kashmir
Nepal
Bhutan
Bangladesh
India
Sri Lanka

Jordan
Kuwait
Bahrain
Qatar
UAE
Saudi Arabia
Yemen
Oman

Maldives
Seychelles

Egypt
Libya
Algeria
Mali
Niger
Chad
Sudan
Eritrea
Djibouti
Somalia
Ethiopia

Mauritania
Senegal
Gambia
Guinea-Bissau
Guinea
Sierra Leone
Liberia
Côte d'Ivoire
Ghana
Togo
Benin
Burkina Faso
Nigeria
Cameroon
Equatorial Guinea
São Tomé & Príncipe
Gabon
Congo
Central African Republic
Democratic Republic of Congo

Cape Verde

Uganda
Rwanda
Burundi
Kenya
Tanzania
Malawi
Comoros
Mozambique
Madagascar
Mauritius
Réunion (France)
Zambia
Zimbabwe
Angola
Namibia
Botswana
South Africa
Swaziland
Lesotho

{52}

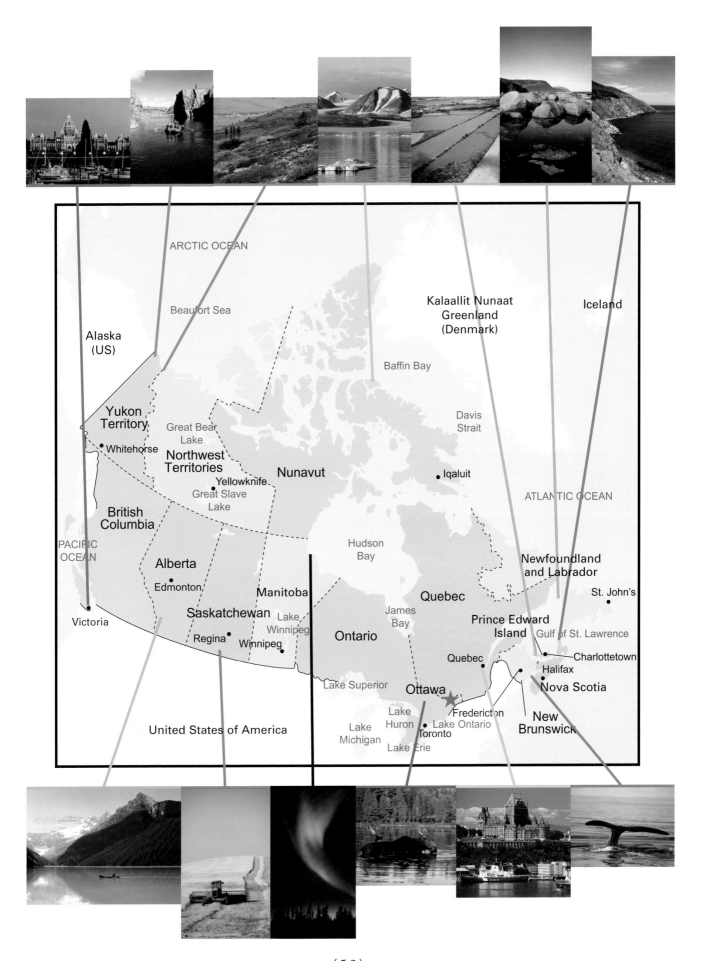

ARCTIC OCEAN

Beaufort Sea

Kalaallit Nunaat
Greenland
(Denmark)

Iceland

Alaska
(US)

Baffin Bay

Yukon
Territory

Davis
Strait

Whitehorse

Great Bear
Lake

Northwest
Territories

Nunavut

Iqaluit

ATLANTIC OCEAN

British
Columbia

Yellowknife

Great Slave
Lake

PACIFIC
OCEAN

Hudson
Bay

Newfoundland
and Labrador

Alberta

St. John's

Edmonton

Manitoba

Quebec

Prince Edward
Island

Gulf of St. Lawrence

Victoria

Saskatchewan

Lake
Winnipeg

James
Bay

Quebec

Charlottetown

Regina

Winnipeg

Ontario

Halifax

Lake Superior

Ottawa

Nova Scotia

United States of America

Lake
Huron

Fredericton

New
Brunswick

Lake
Michigan

Lake Ontario

Toronto

Lake Erie

Make a Book about How Your Family Came to Canada
Your child might be interested in making a scrapbook using words and drawings or photographs about his or her own journey to Canada. What does he or she remember most about the trip? How do the new home and school compare to the old ones? What have the first few weeks and months been like? What has seemed strange or funny? What has been the hardest part? What has been the best part?

For Our Kids is a video featuring nine newcomer parents talking about how they helped their children be successful in school and the importance of parent involvement in the Canadian education system. It is available in 17 languages at www.for-our-kids.ca.

Check your public library for these children's books:

Marianthe's Story: Painted Words and Spoken Memories by Aliki, HarperCollins, 1999.

Out of the Everywhere by Jan Andrews, illustrated by Simon Ng, Groundwood Books, 2000.

Alfredito Flies Home / Alfredito regresa volando a su casa by Jorge Argueta, illustrated by Luis Garay, Groundwood Books, 2007.

Cleversticks by Bernard Ashley, illustrated by Derek Brazell, HarperCollins, 1993.

Nana's Cold Days by Adwoa Badoe, illustrated by Bushra Junaid, Groundwood Books, 2002.

One Green Apple by Eve Bunting, illustrated by Ted Lewin, Clarion Books, 2006.

The Name Jar by Yangsook Choi, Alfred. A Knopf, 2001.

Angel Square by Brian Doyle, Groundwood Books, 1984.

Spud Sweetgrass by Brian Doyle, Groundwood Books, 1992.

Speak English for Us, Marisol! by Karen English, illustrated by Enrique O. Sanchez, Albert Whitman and Company, 2000.

The Lotus Seed by Sherry Garland, illustrated by Tatsuro Kiuchi, Voyager Books, 1997.

The Upside Down Boy / El niño de cabeza by Juan Felipe Herrera, illustrated by Elizabeth Gomez, Children's Book Press, 2000.

The Colour of Home by Mary Hoffman, illustrated by Karin Littlewood, Frances Lincoln, 2002.

I Hate English! by Ellen Levine, illustrated by Steve Bjorkman, Scholastic, 1989.

From Far Away by Robert Munsch, illustrated by Michael Martchenko, Annick Press, 1995.

In English Of Course by Josephine Nobisso, illustrated by Dasha Ziborova, Gingerbread House, 2002.

A Place to Grow by Soyung Pak, illustrated by Marcelino Truong, Scholastic, 2002.

Sumi's First Day of School Ever by Soyung Pak, illustrated by Joung Un Kim, Viking, 2003.

Goodbye, 382 Shin Dang Dong by Frances Park and Ginger Park, National Geographic Society, 2002.

My Name Is Yoon by Helen Recorvits, illustrated by Gabi Swiatkowska, Farrar, Straus & Giroux, 2003.

The Silence in the Mountains by Liz Rosenberg, illustrated by Chris K. Soentpiet, Orchard Books, 1999.

The Chinese Violin by Madeleine Thien, illustrated by Joe Chang, Whitecap Books, 2001.

Suki's Kimono by Chieri Uegaki, illustrated by Stephane Jorisch, Kids Can Press, 2003.

The Sandwich by Ian Wallace, illustrated by Angela Wood, Kids Can Press, 1975.

Ghost Train by Paul Yee, illustrated by Harvey Chan, Groundwood Books, 1996.

Roses Sing on New Snow by Paul Yee, illustrated by Harvey Chan, Groundwood Books, 1991.

Tales from Gold Mountain by Paul Yee, illustrated by Simon Ng, Groundwood Books, 1989.

From THE CANADIAN CHARTER OF RIGHTS AND FREEDOMS

The Canadian Charter of Rights and Freedoms defines the rights and freedoms that Canadians believe are necessary in a free and democratic society. An excerpt from the Charter, including the rights and freedoms, is below.

Whereas Canada is founded upon principles that recognize the supremacy of God and the rule of law:

Guarantee of Rights and Freedoms

1. The *Canadian Charter of Rights and Freedoms* guarantees the rights and freedoms set out in it subject only to such reasonable limits prescribed by law as can be demonstrably justified in a free and democratic society.

Fundamental Freedoms

2. Everyone has the following fundamental freedoms:
   (a) freedom of conscience and religion;
   (b) freedom of thought, belief, opinion and expression, including freedom of the press and other media of communication;
   (c) freedom of peaceful assembly; and
   (d) freedom of association.

Democratic Rights

3. Every citizen of Canada has the right to vote in an election of members of the House of Commons or of a legislative assembly and to be qualified for membership therein.
4. (1) No House of Commons and no legislative assembly shall continue for longer than five years from the date fixed for the return of the writs of a general election of its members.
(2) In time of real or apprehended war, invasion or insurrection, a House of Commons may be continued by Parliament and a legislative assembly may be continued by the legislature beyond five years if such continuation is not opposed by the votes of more than one-third of the members of the House of Commons or the legislative assembly, as the case may be.
5. There shall be a sitting of Parliament and of each legislature at least once every twelve months.

Mobility Rights

6. (1) Every citizen of Canada has the right to enter, remain in and leave Canada.
(2) Every citizen of Canada and every person who has the status of a permanent resident of Canada has the right
   (a) to move to and take up residence in any province; and
   (b) to pursue the gaining of a livelihood in any province.
(3) The rights specified in subsection (2) are subject to
   (a) any laws or practices of general application in force in a province other than those that discriminate among persons primarily on the basis of province of present or previous residence; and

   (b) any laws providing for reasonable residency requirements as a qualification for the receipt of publicly provided social services.
(4) Subsections (2) and (3) do not preclude any law, program or activity that has as its object the amelioration in a province of conditions of individuals in that province who are socially or economically disadvantaged if the rate of employment in that province is below the rate of employment in Canada.

Legal Rights

7. Everyone has the right to life, liberty and security of the person and the right not to be deprived thereof except in accordance with the principles of fundamental justice.
8. Everyone has the right to be secure against unreasonable search or seizure.
9. Everyone has the right not to be arbitrarily detained or imprisoned.
10. Everyone has the right on arrest or detention
   (a) to be informed promptly of the reasons therefor;
   (b) to retain and instruct counsel without delay and to be informed of that right; and
   (c) to have the validity of the detention determined by way of *habeas corpus* and to be released if the detention is not lawful.
11. Any person charged with an offence has the right
   (a) to be informed without unreasonable delay of the specific offence;
   (b) to be tried within a reasonable time;
   (c) not to be compelled to be a witness in proceedings against that person in respect of the offence;
   (d) to be presumed innocent until proven guilty according to law in a fair and public hearing by an independent and impartial tribunal;
   (e) not to be denied reasonable bail without just cause;
   (f) except in the case of an offence under military law tried before a military tribunal, to the benefit of trial by jury where the maximum punishment for the offence is imprisonment for five years or a more severe punishment;
   (g) not to be found guilty on account of any act or omission unless, at the time of the act or omission, it constituted an offence under Canadian or international law or was criminal according to the general principles of law recognized by the community of nations;
   (h) if finally acquitted of the offence, not to be tried for it again and, if finally found guilty and punished for the offence, not to be tried or punished for it again; and

(i) if found guilty of the offence and if the punishment for the offence has been varied between the time of commission and the time of sentencing, to the benefit of the lesser punishment.

12. Everyone has the right not to be subjected to any cruel and unusual treatment or punishment.

13. A witness who testifies in any proceedings has the right not to have any incriminating evidence so given used to incriminate that witness in any other proceedings, except in a prosecution for perjury or for the giving of contradictory evidence.

14. A party or witness in any proceedings who does not understand or speak the language in which the proceedings are conducted or who is deaf has the right to the assistance of an interpreter.

Equality Rights

15. (1) Every individual is equal before and under the law and has the right to the equal protection and equal benefit of the law without discrimination and, in particular, without discrimination based on race, national or ethnic origin, colour, religion, sex, age or mental or physical disability.

(2) Subsection (1) does not preclude any law, program or activity that has as its object the amelioration of conditions of disadvantaged individuals or groups including those that are disadvantaged because of race, national or ethnic origin, colour, religion, sex, age or mental or physical disability.

Official Languages of Canada

16. (1) English and French are the official languages of Canada and have equality of status and equal rights and privileges as to their use in all institutions of the Parliament and government of Canada.

(2) English and French are the official languages of New Brunswick and have equality of status and equal rights and privileges as to their use in all institutions of the legislature and government of New Brunswick.

(3) Nothing in this Charter limits the authority of Parliament or a legislature to advance the equality of status or use of English and French.

16.1. (1) The English linguistic community and the French linguistic community in New Brunswick have equality of status and equal rights and privileges, including the right to distinct educational institutions and such distinct cultural institutions as are necessary for the preservation and promotion of those communities.

(2) The role of the legislature and government of New Brunswick to preserve and promote the status, rights and privileges referred to in subsection (1) is affirmed.

17. (1) Everyone has the right to use English or French in any debates and other proceedings of Parliament.

(2) Everyone has the right to use English or French in any debates and other proceedings of the legislature of New Brunswick.

18. (1) The statutes, records and journals of Parliament shall be printed and published in English and French and both language versions are equally authoritative.

(2) The statutes, records and journals of the legislature of New Brunswick shall be printed and published in English and French and both language versions are equally authoritative.

19. (1) Either English or French may be used by any person in, or in any pleading in or process issuing from, any court established by Parliament.

(2) Either English or French may be used by any person in, or in any pleading in or process issuing from, any court of New Brunswick.

20. (1) Any member of the public in Canada has the right to communicate with, and to receive available services from, any head or central office of an institution of the Parliament or government of Canada in English or French, and has the same right with respect to any other office of any such institution where

(a) there is a significant demand for communications with and services from that office in such language; or

(b) due to the nature of the office, it is reasonable that communications with and services from that office be available in both English and French.

(2) Any member of the public in New Brunswick has the right to communicate with, and to receive available services from, any office of an institution of the legislature or government of New Brunswick in English or French.

21. Nothing in sections 16 to 20 abrogates or derogates from any right, privilege or obligation with respect to the English and French languages, or either of them, that exists or is continued by virtue of any other provision of the Constitution of Canada.

22. Nothing in sections 16 to 20 abrogates or derogates from any legal or customary right or privilege acquired or enjoyed either before or after the coming into force of this Charter with respect to any language that is not English or French.

Minority Language Educational Rights

23. (1) Citizens of Canada

(a) whose first language learned and still understood is that of the English or French linguistic minority population of the province in which they reside, or

(b) who have received their primary school instruction in Canada in English or French and reside in a province where the language in which they received that instruction is the language of the English or French linguistic minority population of the province, have the right to have their children receive primary and secondary school instruction in that language in that province.

(2) Citizens of Canada of whom any child has received or is receiving primary or secondary school instruction in English or French in Canada, have the right to have all their children receive primary and secondary school instruction in the same language.

(3) The right of citizens of Canada under subsections (1) and (2) to have their children receive primary and secondary school instruction in the language of the English or French linguistic minority population of a province

(a) applies wherever in the province the number of children of citizens who have such a right is sufficient to warrant the provision to them out of public funds of minority language instruction; and

(b) includes, where the number of those children so warrants, the right to have them receive that instruction in minority language educational facilities provided out of public funds.